# In Our Neighborhood

# Meet a Mail Carrier!

by Becky Herrick

Illustrations by Lisa Hunt

**Children's Press®**
An imprint of Scholastic Inc.

■ SCHOLASTIC

Library of Congress Cataloging-in-Publication Data
Names: Herrick, Becky, author. | Hunt, Lisa, 1973– illustrator.
Title: Meet a mail carrier!/by Becky Herrick; [illustrations by Lisa Hunt].
Other titles: Meet a mail carrier!
Description: New York: Children's Press, an imprint of Scholastic Inc., [2021]. | Series: In our neighborhood | Includes index. | Audience: Ages 5–7. | Audience: Grades K–1. | Summary: "This book introduces readers to the role of mail carriers in their neighborhood"— Provided by publisher.
Identifiers: LCCN 2020040824 | ISBN 9780531136829 (library binding) | ISBN 9780531136881 (paperback)
Subjects: LCSH: Letter carriers—Juvenile literature. | Postal service—Employees—Juvenile literature.
Classification: LCC HE6241 .H47 2021 | DDC 383/.492—dc23
LC record available at https://lccn.loc.gov/2020040824

Produced by Spooky Cheetah Press
Prototype design by Maria Bergós/Book & Look
Page design by Kathleen Petelinsek/The Design Lab

© 2021 Scholastic Inc.

Printed in North Mankato, MN, USA 113

11/22

1 2 3 4 5 6 7 8 9 10 R 30 29 28 27 26 25 24 23 22 21

Scholastic Inc., 557 Broadway, New York, NY 10012.

Photos ©: 7: Andrew Harrer/Bloomberg/Getty Images; 9: Korbin Berg/Dreamstime; 11: Keith Getter/Getty Images; 13: Pierre Rochon Photography/Alamy Images; 14: Fine Art Images/age fotostock; 17: lucidwaters/age fotostock; 18 left: David R. Frazier Photolibrary, Inc./Alamy Images; 19 left: Greg Mathieson/Mai/The LIFE Images Collection/Getty Images; 19 right: Andreistanescu/Dreamstime; 20: Betty LaRue/Alamy Images; 25: StampCollection/Alamy Images; 31 top right: lucidwaters/age fotostock; 31 bottom left: Betty LaRue/Alamy Images.

All other photos © Shutterstock.

# Table of Contents

# OUR NEIGHBORHOOD

Hi! I'm Theo. This is my best friend, Emma. Welcome to our neighborhood!

gym

courthouse

pharmacy

bank

The Daily Gazette

local newspaper

Supermarket

supermarket

dentist

veterinarian

salon

movie theater

POLICE STATION

police station

construction site

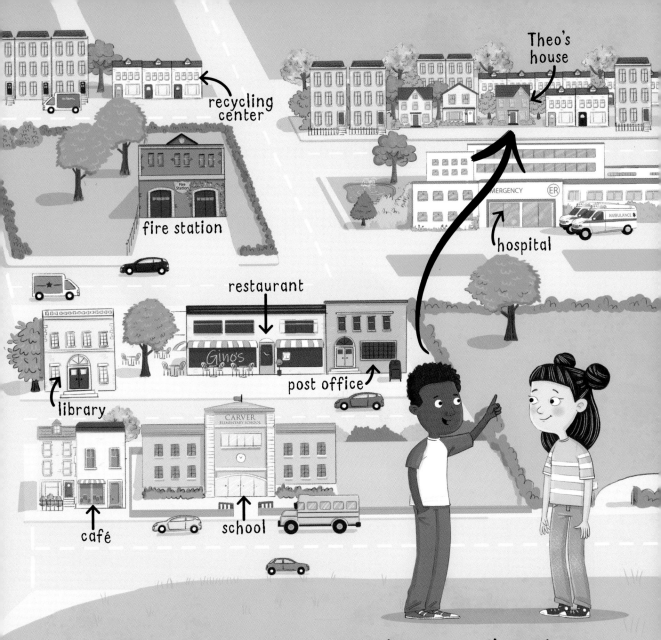

My house is over there. Daniel is the mail carrier for my neighborhood. Last week he brought me a great surprise!

# MEET DANIEL

Emma and I were sitting on my front steps when Daniel pulled up in his mail truck. As he walked up the path, I could see he had lots of mail in his hands.

Hi, Daniel!

Is there any mail for me?

The United States Postal Service (USPS) delivers mail to homes and businesses across the United States.

Daniel handed me some letters and magazines for my parents. Then he gave me a padded envelope. "This one is for you!" he said.

8

Good morning, Mrs. Simmons!

My mom came outside. She gave Daniel a letter to be mailed.

To mail a letter, you need to put a postage stamp on the envelope. This special sticker shows that postage has been paid.

Daniel walked back to his mail truck to put my mom's letter away. The back was filled with a lot of letters, magazines, and boxes. Emma asked Daniel how he keeps all that mail straight.

"I make sure it is sorted and organized before I start my route," Daniel said.

So many letters!

Almost 7,000 mail carriers cover their routes completely on foot. They are called the USPS Fleet of Feet.

Daniel explained how he delivers the mail. "In some areas, houses are close together. I fill my bag and walk up and down each block."

In most mail trucks, the driver sits on the right side instead of the left side. That way, mail can be delivered from the driver's seat!

"In other areas, houses are farther apart. They have mailboxes right by the road. I can deliver mail without getting out of the truck."

Emma and I went inside to open my package.
It was from my cousin Sam! He lives in Michigan.
Sam had sent me a letter and two friendship
bracelets. I gave one to Emma.

The post office was founded in 1775. Benjamin Franklin was the first postmaster general. That's the head of the entire USPS.

# HOW THE MAIL WORKS

The next day, Emma and I went to the store. We saw Daniel taking mail out of a mailbox on the street. "Hi, Daniel!" I said. "Next time you are by my house, can I give you a box to mail to my cousin?"

"Sorry," he said. "That package will need more postage, so you'll have to take it to the post office."

I have a special key.

Letters and small packages can fit in the flap on a mailbox. Only a mail carrier can take them out!

UNITED STATES POSTAL SERVICE

UNITED STATES POSTAL SERVICE

17

"How will the package get from the post office to my cousin's house in Michigan?" I asked.

Daniel said that there is a system in place all across the United States to get mail from one place to another. Then he explained the process.

Mail is taken from the post office to a **processing and distribution center**. Machines and people sort the mail to send it where it needs to go.

Workers put the sorted mail on **trucks**. Some of the mail goes to other processing centers or post offices. Some mail must also travel on **airplanes** to get where it needs to go.

The mail is delivered to the **post office** near its destination. Then it is separated for each of the mail carriers' routes.

**Mail carriers** deliver the mail to homes and businesses.

Wow, there are a lot of steps to get mail from here to there!

That's for sure!

# MAILING OUR PACKAGE

After we made the shirt, my dad helped Emma and me pack it up to send to Sam. We put the shirt in a box and taped it closed.

INTERNAL REVENUE SERVICE
P.O. BOX 802501
CINCINNATI, OH 45280-2501

What's the return address for?

Addresses have zip codes, which are numbers that identify the location. Zip codes allow the mail to be sorted quickly and accurately.

I wrote Sam's address on the front of the box.
Then I added our address in the top left corner.
Dad told me that's called the return address.

So the package can be returned to us if it can't be delivered.

Emma, Dad, and I took our package to the post office. I looked around while we waited. One wall was covered in a lot of tiny doors. I asked my dad what they were. "Those are PO boxes," he said.

People can rent PO boxes inside a post office. Customers have their mail delivered to the boxes instead of to their homes.

Then it was our turn. The clerk weighed our box and told us the cost to send it to Sam. After my dad paid, the clerk handed us a receipt. "This has your tracking number," she said.

Thank you!

ZIP - e/ USPS DELIVERY CONFIRMATION

420 75035 9101 1501 3471 1925 1072 39

Electronic Rate Approved #150134711

A tracking number matches a bar code on a package. You can use that number to go online to find out if the package has been delivered.

Post Office

A few days later, I got a video call from Sam. He got our box! Sam was wearing his new shirt. Emma and I showed him that we were wearing our friendship bracelets.

# Ask a Mail Carrier

Emma asked Daniel some questions about his job.

What kind of training do you need to become a mail carrier?

You have to take an exam, and you need to have a safe driving record. But a lot of learning happens on the job itself!

What do you do when the weather is bad?

I deliver the mail anyway! Mail carriers work in every kind of weather, unless it is truly dangerous. We are out in the heat, rain, slush, and snow.

What is the hardest thing about your job?

There is a lot of mail to deliver every day. When something delays me, it can affect the whole rest of my day. Plus, some of the boxes I deliver can be heavy!

What is something that not everyone might know about the USPS?

Just how big it is! Each day, the Postal Service processes and delivers more than *181* million pieces of mail.

What is your favorite thing about being a mail carrier?

I like providing a service that people need. I also enjoy the conversations I have with customers on my route.

# Daniel's Tips for How to Address an Envelope or Package

- Write with a pen or permanent marker.

- Print the address neatly. Using all capital letters works best. You don't need to include any commas or periods in the address!

- Write the address where you are sending the letter in the center of the envelope. Write your return address in the top left corner.

- Addresses should be written like this, for example:

Theo Simmons
321 Main Street
City State 12345

JOHN SMITH
123 MAIN STREET
COLUMBUS OH 43210

# A Mail Carrier's Tools

**Mailbag:** A mail carrier uses this canvas satchel with a shoulder strap to carry mail.

**Mailbox:** People put letters into this public box to mail them. A mail carrier removes them from the box at certain times during the day.

**Mail truck:** Mail carriers use this vehicle to deliver mail.

**Portable electronic scanner:** Many mail carriers use this device to scan bar codes and track package deliveries.

# Index

# About the Author

Becky Herrick is a writer and an editor who lives in Brooklyn, New York, with her husband, daughter, and cat. She loves getting cards and packages in the mail from family and friends!